A Little Princess

Treasury of Illustrated Classics™

A Little Princess

by
Frances Hodgson Burnett

Adapted by
Tracy Christopher

Illustrated by
Jael
&
Sean Gribbon

Modern Publishing
A Division of Unisystems, Inc.
New York, New York 10022

Series UPC: 39340

Cover art by Julia Lundman

Copyright ©1999, 2002, 2003, 2004, 2005 Kidsbooks, Inc.
230 Fifth Avenue
New York, New York 10001

This edition published by Modern Publishing,
a division of Unisystems, Inc.

Printed in the U.S.A.

Contents

Chapter 1
Sara Crewe

One dark winter's afternoon, a little girl named Sara Crewe found herself rolling through the foggy streets of London, toward a new life at boarding school. She sat in the carriage with her feet tucked under her, and leaned against her father, who held her in his arms. Neither felt much like speaking, because they loved one another very much and were about to part for at least several years.

Sara had been born and raised in India, but she was seven now and her father wanted her to go to school in England. He could not stay with her in London because he was a captain in the British army and had to go back to his soldiers in Bombay. Sara's mother had died when she was very young, so Captain Crewe had had to rely upon a nursemaid in Bombay and now upon a Miss Mary Minchin of Minchin's Select Seminary for Young Ladies to help him raise and educate his daughter.

Sara sat staring out of the carriage window at the passing people. She was a slim, supple girl, rather tall for her age. She had an intense, attractive little face. Sara's hair was heavy and quite long, and curled only at the tips. Her gray-green eyes were very big, and they looked out upon the world with an old-fashioned thoughtfulness that was rather unusual in such a young girl. Sara was thinking that not long ago she and her father had been in India in the blazing sun. Now they were riding in this horse-drawn cab through streets where the day was as dark as the night.

"Papa," Sara said in a voice that was almost a whisper.

"What is it, darling? What is my Sara thinking of?" Ralph Crewe said as he hugged her closer.

"Is this the place? Is it, Papa?"

"Yes, my little Sara, it is. We have reached it at last." He sounded sad as he said it.

"Well, Papa," she said softly. "If we are here, I suppose we must be resigned."

Captain Crewe laughed at this, but he did not feel happy. And he felt less and less resigned once the carriage stopped in front of the big dull brick house that was exactly like all the others in the square. On the front door there shone a brass plate on which was engraved in black letters "Miss Minchin's Select Seminary for Young Ladies."

The house and Miss Minchin seemed exactly alike to Sara as her father led her into the parlor. Both the headmistress and her school were respectable and polished, but stiff and severe—even the armchairs seemed to have hard bones in them. The carpet had a square pattern, the chairs were square, and Miss Minchin herself was rather rectangular, with large, cold eyes and an unfriendly smile.

Sara was to be a parlor-boarder, as Miss Minchin had arranged with Captain Crewe for a larger fee. Sara was to enjoy even greater privileges than parlor-boarders usually did. She was to have a bedroom and a sitting room of her own, and a pony and a carriage. Her personal maid, a Frenchwoman named Mariette, would take care of Sara's clothing and other needs.

Captain Crewe repeated his instructions to Miss Minchin. "Please provide

Sara with as many books as she asks for. She gobbles them as if she were a wolf instead of a little girl. Give her grown-up books—great big, fat ones; French and German as well as English— history and biography and poetry, and all sorts of other books. But you must also make her ride her pony in the park or go out and play when she reads too much. Also, please feel free to provide Sara with every pleasure she asks for. She is a sensible girl, and she rarely wants anything that is not safe or proper to give her. I have told my lawyers, Messieurs Barrow and Skipworth, to pay all the bills you send for Sara's expenses. I will keep in touch with them from Bombay, and I will of course write to my darling girl twice a week."

Then, all of a sudden, it was time to go! Captain Crewe picked up Emily, Sara's doll, and gently put her in Sara's arms, to give his daughter something familiar to hold on to. It occurred to him

that Emily looked almost like a real child, with her golden-brown hair and green eyes. At least Emily would be there to keep Sara company as she got used to all the new people at school. He was certainly going to miss his daughter.

Sara gave her father one last hug. She held the lapels of his army coat in her small hands, and looked long and hard into his face. "Are you learning me by heart, little one?" he asked.

"No, Papa," she answered, "I know you by heart. You are inside my heart." And then she let him get into the cab and drive away. As the carriage disappeared around the corner, Sara could still see Captain Crewe waving and blowing kisses to her as if he could not bear to stop.

"Your father spoils you, my dear. We must hurry to the schoolroom for lessons before the day is quite ended!" Miss Minchin cried as she led Sara into the schoolroom next to the parlor. Once there, she sat Sara down in a desk next to hers and handed her a beginner's book of elementary French. Sara tried to explain that the book was of little interest to her, but Miss Minchin thought she did not want to learn French at all. Just then, the French teacher, Monsieur Dufarge, entered the schoolroom.

"Monsieur Dufarge! Thank goodness you have arrived to help me with this impossible child. She does not want to begin French!" Miss Minchin said, clearly annoyed.

Monsieur Dufarge would understand, thought Sara. She began to explain, in pretty and fluent French—Madame had not understood. Sara's mama had been French, but she had died when Sara was born. Her papa had loved her mama and had wanted Sara to learn her language. So he often spoke French to her, and she had learned to read and write it as well as she could read and write English. She had not learned French out of books, exactly, but she would be glad to learn anything Monsieur Dufarge would like to teach her. It was just that she already knew all the words in the little book Madame Minchin had given her.

"You ought to have told me that your French is perfect!" exclaimed Miss Minchin indignantly as the girls in the schoolroom started to giggle.

"I—I tried. I—I suppose I did not begin quite right."

Miss Minchin knew that Sara had tried to explain and that it had not been her fault that she had not been allowed to speak. But Sara's giggling classmates

made her even more angry. From that moment on, Miss Minchin held a grudge against this new pupil. "Silence, young ladies!" she said severely, rapping upon her desk. "Silence, at once! Ermengarde St. John! Sit down this instant! And take that hair ribbon out of your mouth!"

Sara decided that she would try to be Ermengarde's friend. It was a way of hers to help people who were made to feel uncomfortable or embarrassed or unhappy.

Sara was able to introduce herself to Ermengarde that night at bedtime. As

they talked, Sara learned that Ermengarde's chief trouble in life was that she had a really clever father. If you have a father who knows everything, who speaks seven or eight languages, and who has thousands of books that he has apparently learned by heart, he will probably expect you to be familiar with the contents of your lesson-books. Mr. St. John simply could not understand how a child of his could not manage to excel at history or French or math. It was his firm conviction that Ermengarde must be made to learn, even when she had such trouble memorizing things that she was often in tears at school.

"But don't you love your father more than anything else in the whole world? I do!" Sara exclaimed. Ermengarde's mouth fell open a little at the idea. She knew that it would be far from behaving like a respectable child at a select seminary to say that it had never occurred to her that she could love her father. She was, indeed, greatly embarrassed. "I—I scarcely ever see him," she stuttered. "He is always at work or in his study, reading things."

"I love mine more than all the world ten times over," Sara replied. "That's why I have felt lonely all day. I will probably feel lonely much of the time, now, even when I make new friends like you. My papa has gone away for a long time, you see." Sara put her head against her knees and sat very still, huddled against her loneliness. India was a world away from London, and she missed her father already.

Chapter 2
Becky

Although Sara continued to miss her father, the years at Miss Minchin's passed quickly enough. Sara soon made many friends at school. She was friendly and generous, sharing her possessions and privileges with a free hand. She was motherly toward the younger girls, and never pushed them away or teased them about being so young. Soon she was adored as a goddess by the entire alphabet class, and became the adopted mother of little Lottie Legh, who was considered by most of the older girls to be too young and too spoiled to bother with. Some of these older girls were envious of Sara's clothes and of her popularity, but even they had to admit that this little princess had perfect manners. Sara was charming and unfailingly polite. Her gentle way of saying "please" and "thank you" expressed real appreciation for those around her.

Sara was praised by her teachers for her quickness at her lessons, and for the generosity and friendliness she displayed toward her fellow pupils. Of course, all of the adults at Miss Minchin's were aware of how wealthy Sara was. Consequently, they treated even the simplest thing that Sara did as if it were a virtue. If Sara had not possessed good common sense and a clever mind, she might have become a very self-satisfied, spoiled young lady. Fortunately, she understood a great many things about herself and her circumstances. "Things happen to people by accident," she explained to Ermengarde one day. "It just happened that I have always liked lessons and books, and that I have always been able to remember things as I learned them. Plus, if you have everything you want and everyone is kind to you, how can you help but be good-tempered and pleasant?"

Sara was certainly intelligent and eager to learn, and good-natured about most of the aspects of seminary life at Miss Minchin's. But the greatest talent that Sara possessed was not one that she had a chance to exhibit in the classroom very often. The greatest power Sara possessed was her ability to tell stories and to make everything she talked about seem like the most wonderful event, whether it was wonderful in reality or

not. Sara could fascinate others with her stories, and there was nothing she loved more than telling them. Girls eagerly attended story hour in Sara's room, where they could sit on soft rugs and pillows before a warm fire, amid Sara's books and paintings, and listen with rapt attention. When Sara sat or stood in the midst of a circle of listeners and began to invent wonderful tales, her green eyes grew bigger, her cheeks grew flushed, and, without knowing that she was doing it, she began to act. She made what she told lovely or alarming by the raising or dropping of her voice, by the expressiveness of her body, and by the dramatic movement of her hands. She forgot that she was talking, but rather lived among the fairy folk or the kings and queens whose adventures she was narrating.

One of Sara's favorite subjects for story hour concerned the diamond mines her father had mentioned in his letters. As he explained to Sara, a friend who had been at school with him when he was a boy had unexpectedly come to see him in India. This man was the owner of a large piece of land where diamonds had been found, but he needed money to develop diamond mines. Captain Crewe had agreed to be a partner in his friend's diamond mine venture. Both men were confident that the mines would eventually produce such wealth as made one dizzy to think of. In some letters Sara's father had expressed doubts and worries, since he had given all his money to his friend to invest in this new business. However, he trusted this business partner, and he was as fascinated as Sara was by the idea of diamond mines. To hear Sara tell of the mines at story hour was to hear her invent descriptions of labyrinths of tunnels in the depths of the earth where sparkling stones studded the walls and ceilings, just like those in stories from the *Arabian Nights*.

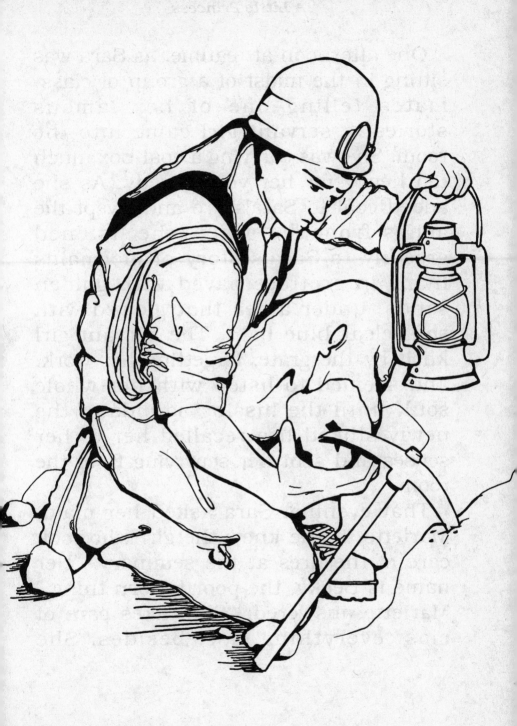

One afternoon at teatime, as Sara was sitting in the midst of a group of class-mates telling one of her famous stories, a servant girl came into the room. She was carrying a coal-box much too heavy for her young body. As she added coal to Sara's fire and swept the ashes from the grate, she listened greedily to Sara's story of mermaids living in grottoes paved with golden sands, under a sea that glowed with soft, clear blue light. The servant girl knelt by the grate, forgetting her work, and seemed to listen with her whole soul, until the hissing sounds of the newly stoked fire recalled her to her senses and sent her scurrying from the room.

That evening, Sara asked her maid, Mariette, if she knew the girl who took care of the fires at the seminary. "Her name is Becky, the poor forlorn thing," Mariette answered. "She takes care of most everything else, besides. She

polishes the grates and carries coal up and down stairs all day. She scrubs the floors and windows and does what the cook and everyone else orders her to do. She is fourteen, I believe, but she never gets enough to eat. That's why she looks no bigger or older than twelve."

Sara vowed that she would try to help Becky. This proved harder than she thought. Becky was so shy that she avoided contact with everyone— especially the girls at the seminary. Sara noticed that whenever anyone spoke to Becky, it seemed as if the poor frightened eyes of the servant girl would jump out of her head. Most of the adults spoke to Becky only to give her something else to do, so that she really had no time to talk even if she had wanted to.

Becky was kept so busy that Sara despaired of ever getting a chance to talk to her at all, much less ask her how she could help. Then one day Sara got lucky. She came back to her room after lunch and found Becky sound asleep in an armchair by the fire. She looked so tired and worn out that Sara could not bear to wake her, so she sat quietly on the rug nearby and waited. Becky woke with a start when a burning lump of coal popped loudly as it fell in the grate.

"Oh, miss! Oh, miss!" Becky stuttered as she clutched wildly at her cap. "I arst your pardon, miss! Oh, I am sorry, miss!"

"Don't be frightened!" Sara answered, smiling reassuringly. "It doesn't matter the least bit!"

"Ain't—ain't yer angry, miss? Ain't yer goin' to tell the missus?"

"No, of course not. Can you stay a few minutes longer? Will Miss Minchin or Cook come looking for you?"

"Here, miss? Me?"

Sara ran to the door and looked out, listening intently. "No one is anywhere about," she explained. "If your bedrooms are finished, perhaps you might stay. I don't want to get you in trouble, but I thought—perhaps—you might like a piece of cake."

That was how the ever-gracious Sara invited Becky to tea. When Becky went downstairs half an hour later, she was not the same girl who had staggered up, loaded down with the weight of the coal-box. She had an extra piece of cake in her pocket. Her cheeks were still warm from Sara's fire, and her child's imagination was still full of the images of the mermaid story that Sara had told all the way to the end just for her.

From that day on, new stories were told in installments during moments Becky could snatch from her days to take tea in Sara's room. Delightful things to eat were tucked into the old-fashioned pocket Becky carried under her skirt, tied around her waist with a band of tape. The search for satisfying things to eat that could be packed away in this pocket like a picnic—meat pies, angel food cake, and the like—added a new interest to Sara's life and a new goal for her trips around town. In time, Becky began to lose her hungry, tired feeling, and the coal-box did not seem so awfully heavy. Even more wonderful were the stories and the friendship—help and comfort and laughter—that Sara provided in Becky's hard-driven young life.

Chapter 3

A Birthday
To Remember

As Sara's eleventh birthday approached, Captain Crewe's letters to his daughter spoke of two subjects close to his heart. The first—his plans for making sure that Sara's eleventh birthday would be the best ever—seemed to fill his heart with delight. The second—his involvement in the diamond mines—seemed to weigh heavily on his mind. He was also struggling with a bad case of Indian marsh fever that kept him in bed feeling tired and weak.

In her most recent letter to her father, written on the morning of her birthday, Sara expressed her hope that he was feeling 100 percent better. Then she answered the question he had asked in his most recent letter to her, namely whether the new doll he had ordered for her in Paris would prove an acceptable birthday present.

"I am getting very old, Papa," Sara wrote as she set down her thoughts to her father on this grand occasion. "You see, after age eleven I will be too old for dolls, so I shall never have another doll given to me at that point. This doll you

are sending will no doubt be my last doll. There is something serious and solemn about it. If I could write poetry, I am sure that a poem about "A Last Doll" would be very nice. But I cannot write poetry. I have tried, and the poem was so awful, it made me laugh. No one could ever take Emily's place, since she was the first doll I had at Miss Minchin's. But I shall respect your new Last Doll very much, and I am sure that the other girls at school will love to play with it. They all like dolls—although some of the bigger girls, the almost-fifteen ones—pretend that they are too grown up for dolls."

By the time that Sara had finished and sealed her birthday letter to her darling papa, it was time to go downstairs for her party. When Sara entered the holly-hung schoolroom, she did so as the head of a sort of procession. Miss Minchin, wearing her grandest silk dress, led her by the hand.

A Little Princess

A manservant followed, carrying the box containing the Last Doll. A housemaid carried a second box, and Becky brought up the rear, carrying a third box and wearing a clean apron and a new cap.

"Now, young ladies, I have a few words to say to you," Miss Minchin began as she looked at all her schoolgirls gathered for Sara's party. "You are aware, young ladies, that Sara is eleven years old today. Several of you here have also been eleven years old, but Sara's birthdays are rather different from those of other little girls. When she is older, she will be the heiress to a large fortune, which it will be her duty to spend in a proper manner."

Sara felt herself growing rather hot from embarrassment. When Miss Minchin talked about money, Sara felt somehow that she hated this woman—and it was, of course, disrespectful to hate grown-up people.

"When her dear papa, Captain Crewe, brought Sara from India and gave her into my care," Miss Minchin continued, "he said to me, in a jesting way, 'I am afraid that Sara will be very rich, Miss Minchin.' My reply to him was, 'Sara's education at my seminary, Captain Crewe, shall be such as will adorn the largest fortune.'" Would Miss Minchin never stop talking? "Sara has become my most accomplished pupil," Miss Minchin droned on. "Her French and her dancing are a credit to the seminary. Her manners are perfect. Her amiability she demonstrates by giving you this afternoon's party. I hope you appreciate her generosity. I wish you to express your appreciation of it by saying aloud all together, 'Thank you, Sara!'"

The entire schoolroom rose to its feet. "Thank you, Sara!" it said, as Lottie Legh began jumping up and down excitedly.

Sara looked rather shy for a moment. She made a curtsy—and it was a very nice one. "Thank you for coming to my party," she replied.

"Very pretty, indeed, Sara," approved Miss Minchin. "Now, I will leave you all to enjoy yourselves."

The instant Miss Minchin swept out of the room, the spell of shyness and discomfort was broken. There was a general rush toward the birthday boxes. Sara bent over the second one with a delighted face. "These are books, I can tell by looking," she said.

"Does your papa send you books for your birthday?" Ermengarde asked in alarm. "Why, he's as bad as my father. Don't open them, Sara!"

"I like books," Sara said, laughing, as she turned to the biggest box. When she took out the Last Doll, it was so magnificent that all the children moved back to gaze at it in breathless rapture.

"She is almost as big as Lottie!"

"She is dressed for the theater! Her cloak is lined with real silk!"

"Here is her trunk. Let's open it and look at all her clothes and things!"

Sara sat down upon the floor and turned the key, then lifted tray after tray from the trunk to reveal its contents. Never had the schoolroom been in such an uproar. In the trunk there were hand-knit lace collars and silk stockings and miniature embroidered handkerchiefs. There was a jewel-case that contained a necklace and a tiara for the doll that looked as if they were made of real diamonds. There were hand-sewn ball gowns and walking dresses and visiting dresses. There were hats and tea gowns and fans, and a pair of blue-and-gold enameled opera glasses!

"Suppose," Sara said as she put a large black velvet hat on the Last Doll, "suppose she understands human talk and feels proud of being admired."

"You are always pretending things," her classmate Lavinia teased her rather meanly.

"I know I am," answered Sara. "I like it. There is nothing quite as nice as supposing. It is almost like being a fairy godmother. If you suppose something hard enough, it seems as if it were real."

"It is all very well to suppose things, if you have everything," Lavinia said spitefully, envious of Sara's doll. "Could you suppose and pretend just as well if you were a beggar and lived in an attic?"

Sara stopped arranging the Last Doll's ostrich plumes, and looked thoughtful. "I believe I could," she replied. "If I were a beggar, I would have to suppose and pretend all the time. It certainly would not be easy."

Sara often thought afterward how strange it was that just as she had finished saying this—just at that very moment—Miss Amelia, Miss Minchin's sister, came into the schoolroom. "Sara," she said, "your father's lawyer has just come to see Miss Minchin. Since she must talk to him alone and since the refreshments are already laid out in our parlor, you girls must come in and have your feast now, so that the schoolroom is available for their discussion."

Chapter 4

Newly Orphaned

When Miss Minchin came out of the schoolroom, after her conversation with Mr. Barrow, she was deathly pale and very, very angry. "Where is Sara Crewe?" she demanded of the bewildered Miss Amelia.

"Why, she is with the other children in our parlor, of course."

"Does she have a black dress in her elegant wardrobe?" Miss Minchin asked with a strange, sneering tone to her voice.

"A black dress?" Miss Amelia stammered. "A black one?"

"She has frocks of every other color and description. Does she not have a black one?"

Miss Amelia turned pale. "Ye—es!" she said fearfully. "But it is too short for her. She has only the old black velvet, and she has outgrown it."

"Go tell her to take off that pink party dress and put on the black one, whether it is too short or not. Sara Crewe is through with fine things!" Miss Minchin said curtly.

Miss Amelia began to wring her hands and cry. "Oh, dear sister!" she wailed. "What on earth has happened!"

Miss Minchin wasted no words. "Captain Crewe is dead," she said flatly. "He has died without a penny. He has no relatives, no one who will take the child. Our pampered parlor-boarder has been left an orphan and a pauper, a burden on our hands!"

Miss Amelia sat down quite heavily in the nearest chair.

"Hundreds of pounds have I spent on this birthday nonsense for her," Miss Minchin said angrily. "Money he was supposed to repay me! And now I shall never see a shilling of the debt she owes me. Go put an end to this ridiculous party of hers. Go make her change her dress this instant!"

When her older sister spoke in such a manner, the best thing to do was obey without question or comment. Miss Amelia slipped out of the room to break up the festivities across the hall.

Miss Minchin had never looked quite so rectangular and hard as she did when Sara came to see her at her bidding a few hours later, in the parlor. By that time it seemed to Sara as if the birthday party had been a dream. A dream or an event that had happened years ago, in the life of another little girl. Sara stood before Miss Minchin, her face white but her eyes dry. Her eyes had dark rings around them, and her mouth was set as if she did not wish her features to reveal what she had suffered, and was suffering. She had put on the black velvet frock. It was too short and tight, making her slender legs look

overly long and thin beneath the skirt. She had not been able to find a piece of black ribbon, so her thick black hair tumbled around her face. She held Emily tightly in one arm, and had wrapped the doll in a piece of black material.

"Put down your doll," Miss Minchin ordered. "What do you mean by bringing it in here?"

"I will not put her down," Sara answered bravely. "Emily is all I have. My papa gave her to me."

"You will have no time for dolls in your future here at the seminary. You are a charity case now. You will have to work to make yourself useful around here."

Sara kept her big, staring eyes fixed upon Miss Minchin, but said not a word. If she had cried out or sobbed, or seemed frightened, then Miss Minchin might have softened somewhat, since she was principally a woman who liked to feel her power over others. However,

as she looked at Sara's pale little steadfast face, Miss Minchin felt her power dwindle away.

"Do not put on airs, young lady," Miss Minchin snapped. "The time for that sort of thing is past. You'll not live here as a little princess any longer. Your carriage and pony will be sold. Your maid will be dismissed. You will wear your oldest and plainest clothes—the rest are no longer appropriate and will be sold. From now on you will be another Becky—you will work for your food and lodging here. You will sleep in the attic, in the room next to Becky's. You will do whatever you are told to do by any of the staff at this seminary. You will run errands and you will help in the kitchen as well as in the schoolroom, supervising the lessons of the youngest children. If you do not please me, you will be sent away. It is that simple, so keep what I have said in mind at all times. Now go!"

Sara stood still for a moment, looking at the unfeeling woman before her. Then she turned to leave the room.

"Excuse me," Miss Minchin said in a tone meant to stop Sara in her tracks. "Don't you intend to thank me?"

"What for?" Sara replied softly.

"For my kindness to you. For my kindness in giving you a home when you have no other."

Sara took two or three steps toward her tormentor, her thin little chest

heaving up and down as she answered in a strange, fierce voice, "You are not kind. And this is not a home." Sara ran from the room before Miss Minchin could do anything but stare after her in angry amazement.

Chapter 5
Life in
the Attic

The newly orphaned child climbing the two flights of stairs to the attic, wearing her short black dress, was quite different from the girl who had celebrated her birthday just hours before. Sara felt as if she were walking away and leaving far behind the world in which that other child, who no longer seemed herself, had lived. When she reached the attic door and opened it, her heart gave a dreary little thump. Here was her new home.

Yes, this was indeed another world. This attic room of hers had a slanted roof, so that Sara could not stand up straight unless she stood at one end of it. The whitewash was dingy and had chipped off in places. There was an old iron bedstead with a rock-hard mattress, covered by a faded cotton quilt that would not keep her warm in cold weather. Under the skylight in the roof, which showed nothing but a piece of dull gray sky, there stood a battered red footstool and an old table.

Sara sat down on the hard, cold floor. She did not cry, but she laid Emily across her knees and put her face down upon her doll. She put her arms around her knees and sat there, her head resting on the black mourning cloth of her doll, not making a sound. Becky found her huddled that way late in the evening, when she came up with pieces of her own dinner for Sara, scraps she had hidden in the pocket underneath her dress.

The change in Sara's life was made all at once. "She must begin as she is to go on," Miss Minchin reasoned with Miss Amelia. "She must be taught at once what she is to expect."

"You will begin your new duties this morning, Sara," Miss Minchin instructed the following morning at breakfast. "You will take your seat with the younger

children at the small table. You must
keep them quiet, and you must see that
they behave well. It is especially
important that they not waste food. In
the future, you must come down earlier,
to set the table. And get a towel. Lottie
has spilled her tea."

From that moment on, every day the
duties given to Sara became more
numerous. If she had been older than
eleven, Miss Minchin would have given

her the bigger girls to teach. That way, the headmistress would have replaced a paid instructress with Sara, and she would have forced Sara to work for nothing. She would have saved money on salary. However, as long as Sara remained and looked like a child, she could not be put in charge of the schoolroom. Instead, she would become a sort of superior errand girl and unpaid maid of all work. An ordinary errand boy was not as clever and as reliable as Sara, who could be trusted with difficult tasks and complicated messages. She could be told to do things other people neglected or had no time for. She could even go pay bills. Yet she combined this level of trustworthiness and this sense of responsibility with the skill necessary to dust and straighten up rooms without breaking things.

The time Sara had once spent in the schoolroom formally pursuing her own education became a thing of the past. She was taught nothing. Only after long and busy days spent running here and there at everyone's orders was she allowed to enter the deserted schoolroom with a pile of books. She

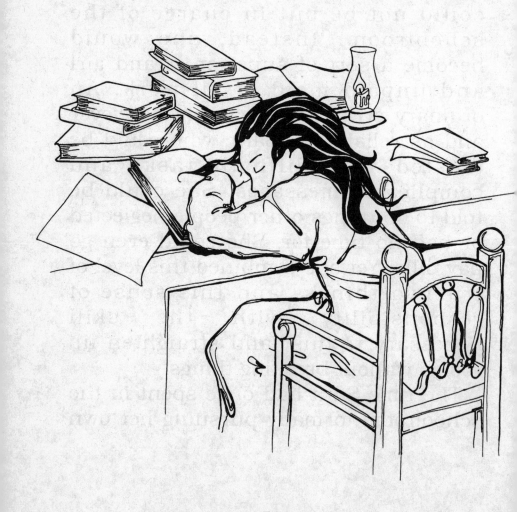

studied alone at night, and sometimes fell asleep over her notebooks.

The only time Sara saw her former classmates was when she was required to supervise the younger children at lessons or at meals. She had no real opportunity to speak to any of the girls her age, and she could not help but see that Miss Minchin preferred her to live a life apart from that of the other students. As Sara's dresses grew shabbier, and as she wore holes in the toes and heels of her old shoes, girls her age in the seminary began to view her as a servant. Finally, her clothes became so ragged that she was told that she had better take her meals downstairs in the kitchen. In short, Sara was treated as if she were nobody's child. Her heart grew sore, but she was too proud to make trouble.

"Soldiers do not complain," Sara told herself between small teeth clamped shut. "I am not going to do it. I will pretend that this is part of a war. I am a prisoner in the enemy's camp. I am a prisoner in the Bastille prison!" Nevertheless, there were hours when her child's heart seemed ready to break from loneliness and fatigue.

Sara's heart might indeed have broken were it not for the presence of three people in her life. First, there was Becky, who lived next door—a fellow prisoner in what Sara thought of as the infamous French prison, the Bastille. Then there was Ermengarde, who began sneaking up to Sara's attic room at night, after everyone fell asleep, to keep her company. Finally, there was Lottie, who found her way up to Sara's attic room one afternoon and almost burst out crying at the ugliness of Sara's new home.

"Sara!" Lottie cried, aghast. "Mama Sara!"

Sara jumped down from her place at the skylight and ran to the child. "Please don't cry and make noise," she implored. "I shall be scolded if you do, and I have been scolded all day today. It's—it's not such a bad room, Lottie."

"It's not? Why isn't it, Sara?" Lottie whispered.

Sara hugged her close and tried to laugh. There was a sort of comfort in the warmth of Lottie's plump, childish body. Sara had had a hard day and had been staring out of the skylight with hot, tear-filled eyes.

"You can see all sorts of things you cannot see from the lower floors downstairs," Sara explained.

"What sort of things?" Lottie asked with a newfound curiosity that Sara could awaken in children, even in girls older than herself, and certainly in younger girls like Lottie.

"Chimneys—quite close to us—with smoke curling up in wreaths, and clouds going up into the sky, and sparrows hopping about on the roofs

and talking to one another just as if they were people, and other attic windows like mine. And it all feels so high up—as if it were another world."

"Oh, let me see it!" cried Lottie. "Lift me up!"

Sara lifted her up. They stood on the old table together, leaned on the edge of the flat skylight in the roof, and looked out. The sky seemed so much nearer than when one saw it from the streets of London. Lottie was enchanted.

"When the morning begins to sneak into my room from this window," Sara recounted, "I can lie in bed and look right up into the sky. If the sun is going to shine, little pink clouds float about, and I feel as if I could touch them. And if it rains, the drops patter and patter as if they were saying something nice to me. And if there are stars, you can lie and try to count how many go into the patch of night framed by the window. You see, it is really a beautiful little room."

"Oh, Sara!" cried Lottie. "I should like to live here, too!"

When the two girls had finished their tour of the room, Sara persuaded Lottie to go back downstairs, before Miss Minchin discovered she was missing. After sending Lottie on her way, Sara stood in the middle of her attic room and looked around her again. The

enchantment of her imagining for Lottie had died away. The mere fact that Lottie had come and gone away again made things seem a little worse—in the same way prisoners probably feel a little more depressed after visitors have come and gone, leaving them behind. "This is a lonely place," Sara said to herself. "Sometimes, it is the loneliest place in the world."

Chapter 6

The Indian Gentleman

One winter morning, as Sara exited the seminary to begin her first round of errands, she stopped short at the sight of a large moving van pulled up at the curb of the town house next door. The front doors of the house were thrown open, and men in their shirtsleeves were going in and out, carrying heavy boxes and pieces of furniture.

Sara had an idea that she could guess something about the people who had bought the house by looking at their

furniture as it was being unloaded from the van. "Miss Minchin's tables and chairs are just like her," she thought. "I remember thinking that, the first minute I saw her, even though I was only seven. I told Papa, and he laughed and laughed, but he agreed that it was true."

Then Sara saw something that made her heart beat faster in recognition—a beautiful table of elaborately carved teakwood. The table had six matching chairs and a screen covered with rich Oriental embroidery. Sara had seen objects like these when she had lived in India. The sight of them now, set down in the streets of London, gave her a weird, homesick feeling. One of the things Miss Minchin had taken from her and sold was a carved teakwood desk that her father had sent her. The table being carried into the house reminded her of that desk.

"What beautiful things," she said. "They look as if they ought to belong to people with excellent taste. Everything looks rather grand and expensive. I suppose it is a wealthy family that is moving in next door. I wonder if they have children."

Moving vans continued to arrive and be unloaded all day long. Several times it so happened that Sara had the opportunity of seeing things carried in. It became plain that she had been right in guessing that the newcomers were people of considerable means. All the furniture was well-made and beautiful. A great deal of it had clearly been purchased in the Orient. Wonderful rugs and draperies and decorative ornaments were taken into the house. There were dozens of paintings and prints, and books enough for a large library. Among these things, Sara noticed a superb statue of the Buddha, housed in a splendid shrine.

"Someone in the family must have lived in India," Sara mused. "They have grown accustomed to Indian things and

like them. I am glad they are moving next door. I shall feel as if they are friends, even if we never happen to meet."

Just then, a carriage pulled up near the place where Sara was standing. It stopped in front of the house directly across the square from the seminary. This was the Large Family's house and carriage. Sara quickly shifted her attention to the front door of the Large Family's house, in anticipation of some happy event.

Of course, Sara had no idea what the real name of what she called the Large Family might be. She had invented her name for them not because the members of the family were big. Indeed, most of them were little. She had dubbed them the Large Family because there were so many of them in one large house. There were eight children, in addition to a mother and father and grandmother. There were also several nannies and servants living in the house.

The eight children were always being taken out to walk or ride, or flying to the front door in the evening to greet their papa. Or they were crowding about the nursery windows and looking out and laughing. In fact, the members of the Large Family were always doing something enjoyable and suited to the tastes of a large, monied family.

Sara was so fond of observing them that she had given the children names out of books—quite romantic names. She called them the Montmorencys, when she did not call them the Large Family. The fat baby with the lace cap was Ethelberta Beauchamp Montmorency. The little boy who could just barely walk and who had such round legs was Sydney Cecil Vivian Montmorency. Then came Lilian Evangeline, Maud Marion, Rosalind Gladys, Guy Clarence, Veronica Eustacia, and Claude Harold Hector.

And now, with their carriage waiting at their front door, it seemed to Sara that several of the Montmorency children were leaving the house for a children's party. The girls, wearing white lace frocks with lovely satin sashes under

warm coats, ran out of the house and into the carriage, squabbling for the best seats. Guy Clarence followed more slowly, since he was only about five and was carrying a small wrapped gift very carefully in one hand.

Sara was busy thinking about how cute little Guy Clarence was, with his darling round head covered with curls. She did not realize that Guy Clarence had noticed her standing there in her shabby dress and patched coat. Guy Clarence must have thought that Sara looked hungry. He did not know that what she really longed for was the warm, merry life his home held. He only saw Sara's thin face and thin legs and staring eyes and poor clothes. So, he put his hand in his pocket and took out a new sixpence, the one he had just received for Christmas, and held it out to her. "Here, poor little girl," he said. "Here is my sixpence. I will give it to you."

All at once, Sara realized that she looked to Guy Clarence exactly like the children of poor families that she had seen, in the days when her father was alive, waiting on the sidewalk to watch her get out of her carriage. And she had given these children coins many a time. Sara blushed bright red. For a second she felt as if she could not possibly bring herself to take the sixpence from that dear little hand.

"Oh, no!" she cried. "Oh, no, thank you! I must not take it, indeed!"

But Guy Clarence was not to be defeated in his act of charity. He thrust the sixpence into Sara's hand. "Yes, you must take it, poor little girl!" he insisted. "You can buy things to eat with it. It is a whole sixpence."

There was something so sincere and touching in his face, and he looked so likely to be heartbroken if she did not take his coin, that Sara realized she must not refuse him. To act as proud as that would be a cruel thing to do to Guy Clarence.

"Thank you, my dear sir," Sara said sweetly. "You are a kind, sweet, darling, generous boy." And as Guy Clarence scrambled joyfully into the carriage, Sara hurried back to the seminary, trying to smile, although her eyes were shining through a mist of tears. She had known that she looked odd and shabby, but until that moment she had not known that she might be taken for a beggar.

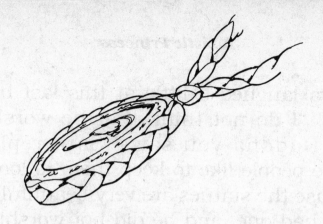

At the end of the day, Becky found her fellow prisoner of the Bastille in her attic cell, wrapping a new sixpence in a piece of narrow ribbon.

"What's that for?" Becky asked.

"It is a keepsake. I am making a necklace with it," Sara answered simply.

"It's an Indian gentleman that's comin' to live next door, miss," Becky said in her peculiar servant's slang. She watched Sara braiding the ribbon around the coin. "He's very rich, but he's ill, an' the father of your Large Family is his lawyer. He's had a lot of trouble, an' it's made him ill an' low in his mind, all depressed-like. He worships idols, miss. I seen an idol bein' carried in for him to worship. It was a statue of a man wearin' a robe."

Sara laughed a little at this last bit of news. "I do not think that he worships that Buddha you saw," Sara replied. "Some people like to keep them to look at because the statues are very beautiful. My papa had one, and he did not worship it. He thought it was interesting."

Becky was inclined to believe that the new neighbor was a worshiper of idols, a heathen pure and simple. It sounded so much more romantic. Who wanted to think of the gentleman from India as a mere ordinary gentleman, born in England and back in London to sit in church with a prayer book? "I never lived next door to heathens, miss," Becky said excitedly. "I should like to see what sort o' ways this gentleman has."

Chapter 7

Princess of the Bastille

"**T**here is one truly nice thing about being a prisoner of the Bastille," Sara thought as she gazed out her attic window at the evening sky. "I have the only room in the whole seminary to have such a splendid view of London's sunsets."

When the light began to glow in a mysterious way in the square, Sara knew that something wonderful was going on in the sky above. When it was at all possible to leave the kitchen without being missed or called back, she crept away and up the flights of stairs to her attic room. Climbing on the old table, Sara would open the skylight and stick her head and body as far out the window as possible. Then she would take a deep breath and look all around her. She had the sky and the entire top of the world to herself. No one else ever looked out of other attic windows, as far as Sara could tell.

Quite alone at her window, Sara would stand, sometimes turning her face upward to the blue sky, which seemed so friendly and near. Sometimes she watched the west and all the wonderful

things that happened there—the clouds drifting, waiting to be softly painted pink or red or purple or pale dove-gray. There were places in the clouds where it seemed that Sara could run or climb or stand and wait to see what else was coming, until it all melted, and she could float back down to earth. Nothing had ever seemed quite so beautiful to Sara as the things she saw as she stood on the table—her body half out of the skylight—the sparrows twittering with sunset softness on the roof tile slates around her.

There was a spectacular sunset a few days after the English gentleman back from India and his manservant had moved in next door. Sara had finished her afternoon's work in the kitchen, so she was able to slip away and head upstairs. She got up on her table and stood looking west. It was a wonderful moment. There were floods of liquid gold covering the western sky, as if a glorious tide had swept over the world. A deep, rich yellow light filled the air. The birds flying across the tops of London's houses showed quite black against the skyline.

"It is a splendid one," Sara said softly to herself. "It makes me feel almost afraid—as if something strange were going to happen. The splendid ones always make me feel that way."

Sara turned her head as she heard a sound a few yards away, in the direction of the town house next door. It was an odd sound, like a queer little squeaky chattering. It came from the window of the next attic. Someone had finally come to look at the sunset, as she was doing.

A head emerged from the skylight next door, the white-turbaned head of a native of India. The squeaky sound Sara heard came from a small monkey that peeked up out of the window a few seconds later.

The first thing Sara thought was that this man looked homesick. She felt sure he had come up to the roof to look at the sun because he had seen the sun so seldom in England that he really missed the light and warmth it had provided in India. Sara smiled and waved from across the slate tiles of the roof. She had learned how comforting even a mere polite nod or smile could be.

The friendly look in Sara's eyes was always effective when people felt tired or dully depressed. The manservant's whole expression changed as he smiled back. It was as if the light had suddenly shone full upon his face and gleamed from his perfect white teeth. As he waved a return greeting, the monkey he was holding slipped from his arms and jumped onto the slates.

He rested there for a moment, and then jumped down into Sara's room.

Sara laughed delightedly at the monkey's playfulness, but she realized that it might be difficult to catch this creature. She spoke to the man from India in his native language, glad that she was able to remember some of the Hindustani she had learned when she was very young. "Excuse me, sir, but do you

think your monkey will let me catch him,
so that I can return him to you?" Sara
asked in Hindustani.

Delighted at the sound of the language
he understood best, the man
quickly introduced himself. First, he
complimented Sara on her ability to
speak his language so well and so
prettily. His name was Ram Dass. He
was the servant of the English
gentleman who was ill. The monkey was
a good monkey and would not bite, but
he would be difficult to catch. This
monkey was disobedient, and would run
from the young lady, and he could jump
like lightning. Ram Dass knew him as if
he were his child. The monkey would
sometimes obey Ram Dass, but not
always. If the young lady would permit
it, Ram Dass would cross the roof to her
room, where he could enter the window
and capture the unworthy little animal.

"Are you able to get across the roof?"
Sara asked. Ram Dass nodded, smiling

broadly. "Then come," she said. "Your poor monkey is flying from side to side in my room, as if he is frightened. Oh, and please allow me to introduce myself—my name is Sara."

Ram Dass crossed the two roofs as steadily and as speedily as if he walked ninety feet off the ground all his life. Once inside, he bowed to Sara formally. The monkey cried out as soon as he saw his owner. It was not a very long chase. The monkey prolonged it for a few minutes simply for the fun of it, but eventually jumped onto Ram Dass's shoulder and sat there, clinging to his neck with his weird, skinny arms.

Ram Dass thanked Sara again for her kindness. She had seen his quick eyes take in at a glance all the bare shabbiness of her room, but he spoke to her as if he were speaking to the daughter of an Indian prince. "This little evil one," he said, stroking the monkey, "is not as evil as he might seem. My master, the English gentleman, is sometimes amused by him. He might perhaps have become even more sad

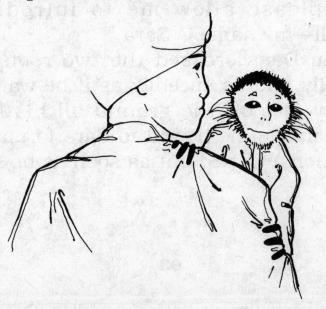

and depressed if his favorite pet animal had run away and gotten lost."

Ram Dass bowed to Sara once more in gratitude and left through the skylight with as much grace and physical agility as the monkey himself had displayed. Once her visitors had departed, Sara stood in the middle of her room and thought of the past. It seemed a strange thing to remember that she—the drudge to whom the cook had said insulting things an hour before—had once been surrounded by people who all treated her as respectfully as Ram Dass had treated her. The past was sort of like a dream. It was all over, and it could never come back. It certainly seemed that there was no way in which change for the better could take place.

Sara stood quite still for several minutes, thinking over her future. Then a thought came that made the color rise in her cheeks and a spark light in her eyes. She straightened her thin little body and lifted her head. "Whatever comes," she said defiantly, "it cannot alter one thing. I may not look like a princess, dressed in rags and tatters, but I can still remain a princess inside. It would be easy to be a princess if I were dressed in cloth of gold, but a greater triumph lies in remaining kind and generous and noble toward those who see me only in my rags and tatters. I will not stoop to being rude to those who are unkind or vulgar, because they do not know any better. A princess must remain polite at all times. She must not become mean-spirited like others around her."

After reminding herself of her true inner identity, the princess of the Bastille went back downstairs. When the servants, taking their tone from Miss Minchin, ordered her about, Sara held her head up and replied so politely that it made them stare at her in amazed confusion. During the final rush to get

dinner ready that evening, even the cook
was forced to admit to the principal
housemaid, "That girl Sara's got more
airs and graces than if she'd come from
Buckingham Palace. I lose my temper
often enough, I know, but I have to
admit that Sara never forgets her
manners, even when I do. 'If you please,
Cook?' 'Will you be so kind, Cook?' 'I beg
your pardon, Cook!' 'May I trouble you,
Cook?' Why, she drops polite speeches
around the kitchen as if they were
second nature to her!"

Chapter 8

The Silver Fourpence

The cold and wet days of winter made the muddy streets of London all the worse for those who had to spend a lot of time in them. There were days when the fog was so thick that the streetlamps remained lit all day and Sara's breath hung in clouds in the cold, damp air. On such days, the windows of the house of the Large Family across the square always looked delightfully cozy and welcoming. And the study of the town house next door to the seminary, where the Indian gentleman sat wrapped in blankets before a blazing fire, glowed with warmth and rich color.

It was certainly miserable weather outside, though, and Sara found herself out in it all day on one particularly bad day. The streets were chilly and sloppy and full of a dull, cold mist. There was mud everywhere—sticky, smelly, London

mud—oozing over and in through the
holes and soles of Sara's thin boots.
Drizzling rain had soaked through the
few layers of clothes Sara was still able
to wear, and she had to walk really fast
to keep from shivering. As she struggled
through the muddy streets, Sara tried to
make her mind think of something
besides how cold and hungry she felt.

"Suppose I had new, dry, well-fitting
clothes," Sara mumbled to herself.
"Suppose I had good boots and a long,
thick coat, and wool stockings, and
gloves, and an umbrella. And suppose—
suppose—just when I was near a bakery
where they sold hot buns, I happened to
find a sixpence in the street that
belonged to nobody. Suppose, if I did
find a sixpence, then I could go into the
shop and buy six of those buns, hot from
the oven, and I could eat them all without
stopping."

Sara was crossing the street as she
said this. The mud was awful—she

almost had to wade through it. She picked her way as carefully as she could, but she could not save herself much. However, in picking her way, she had to look down at her feet and the muddy street. In looking down—just as she reached the boardwalk on the other side—she saw something shining in the gutter. It was a piece of silver—a tiny piece, trodden upon by many feet, but it still shone a little. Not quite a sixpence, but the next best thing to it—a fourpenny piece.

In one second the fourpence was in Sara's cold little hand. "Oh," she gasped. "It is true! I am holding it in my hand!" Then, as Sara looked up from her hand clutching the fourpence, she realized that she was looking straight at the shop directly facing her—a baker's shop! A cheerful, motherly woman with big rosy cheeks was putting into the window a tray of newly baked hot buns, fresh from the oven—large, plump, delicious buns, with currants in them.

The sight of the bakery and the hot buns made Sara feel almost faint for a few seconds. She experienced the shock of a wish come true, and the delightful

odor of warm bread floating up through the baker's cellar window. Sara knew that the money was hers to spend. The coin had been lying in the mud for some time, and its owner was completely lost in the stream of passing people. It was only a very small coin, hardly worth anything to most people, anyway.

"But I'll go ask the baker woman if she has lost anything," Sara said aloud. As she put her wet foot on the step leading to the door of the bakery, she saw something that made her stop. It was a little figure, more forlorn even than she was— a little girl who seemed not much more than a bundle of rags, from which small, bare, red, muddy feet peeped out, only because the rags with which their owner was trying to cover them were not long enough.

Big, hollow, hungry eyes stared up at Sara as the child shuffled to one side of the step to give Sara room to pass. She looked like she was used to being

made to give room to everybody. If a policeman happened to see her, he would no doubt make her move on, away from the shop altogether.

Sara clutched her fourpenny piece and spoke to the child on the steps. "You are hungry, aren't you?" she asked.

"Ain't I just," the girl answered in a voice hoarse with cold. "Just ain't I!"

"You haven't had any dinner?"

"No dinner—nor yet no breakfast nor yet no supper. No nothin'."

"Since when? When did you last eat?" Sara asked.

"Dunno. Never got nothin' today—nowhere. I've asked and asked."

Just to look at the child made Sara

more hungry and faint. But those queer little thoughts were at work in her brain, and she was talking silently to herself. "If I am truly a princess," Sara thought, "then I must share. Because princesses, when they were poor and driven from their thrones—they always shared—if they met someone poorer and hungrier than they were. They always shared. Buns are a penny each. It won't be enough food for either of us. But it will be better than nothing at all."

"Wait a minute for me here," Sara said aloud to the beggar child as she went into the bakery. The shop was warm and smelled wonderful. The baker woman was just going to put more hot buns into the window display.

"If you please, ma'am," Sara said, "have you lost fourpence—a silver fourpence?" She held the little coin out to her for inspection.

The woman looked at it and then at Sara—at her cold, pinched face and her ragged clothes. "Bless us! No," she answered. "Did you find it?"

"Yes," Sara replied, "Out there, in the gutter, in front of your shop."

"Keep it, then. It may have been there for a week, and goodness knows who might have lost it. You could never find out."

"I thought I would ask, first."

"Not many would ask," said the woman, looking puzzled and interested and friendly all at once. "Would you like

something?" she added, as she saw Sara glance hungrily at the buns.

"Yes, ma'am. Four buns, if you please," she said. "The ones at a penny each."

The woman went to the window and put some into a paper bag. Sara noticed that she put in six.

"Only four, please," Sara reminded her. "I have only fourpence."

"Today's special," said the woman, with a good-natured wink. "I dare say you can eat them all sometime. You look like you'd have a good appetite."

A mist rose in Sara's eyes, making it hard to see through the forming tears. "I am much obliged to you for your kindness," she replied thankfully.

Sara was about to tell the lady about the child on the steps, when three customers entered the shop and the baker woman had to hurry to serve them. So Sara merely called out her good-byes and left the bakery.

Outside, Sara opened the paper bag

and took out one of the hot buns, which was so warm that it had already warmed her own hands a little. "Look," she said, placing the bun in the ragged lap of the beggar child, "this is nice and hot. Eat it, and you won't feel so terribly hungry anymore."

The child stared up at Sara as if such sudden, amazing good luck almost frightened her. Then she snatched up the bun and began stuffing it into her mouth with great wolfish bites. "Oh, my!

Oh, my!" Sara heard her exclaim in wild delight. "Oh, my!"

The sound of the ravenously hungry voice was awful. Sara took out three more buns, and put them in the girl's lap. "She is much hungrier than I am," Sara thought to herself. "She is starving." But her hand trembled as she set down the fourth bun of the six. "I am not starving," Sara reminded herself firmly—and she put down a fifth bun in the child's lap.

"Good-bye!" Sara called back as she moved away, across the street. When she turned to look back and wave once more, the child had taken a bun in each hand and had stopped in the middle of a bite to look in amazement at her. Sara gave her a little nod, and the child, after another stare—a curious, lingering stare—jerked her shaggy head in response. Until Sara was out of sight, she did not take another bite.

The child was still eating buns when

the baker woman happened to look out the window. "Well, I never!" she exclaimed. "If that young one hasn't given her buns to a beggar child! It certainly wasn't because she didn't want them, either. I'd give something to know what she did it for." She stood behind her window display a few minutes more, and pondered. Then her curiosity made her go to the door and address the beggar child.

"Who gave you those buns?" she demanded.

The child nodded her head toward Sara's vanishing figure.

"She asked me if I was 'ungry."

"What did you say to her?"

"Said ain't I just."

"And then she came in and got the buns, and gave them to you, did she?"

The child nodded yes.

"How many?"

"Five."

The woman thought it over. "Left just one for herself," she said in a low voice. "And she could have eaten the whole six—I saw it in her eyes." The baker woman looked at the bedraggled figure of Sara moving far away down the street. She felt more disturbed than she had felt in many a day.

"I wish she hadn't gone so quickly," she said. "I should have given her a dozen." Then she turned to the child on the steps. "Are you still hungry?" she asked.

"I'm allus 'ungry, but it ain't so bad as it was."

"Come inside and have some soup," said the baker woman, and she held open the bakery door.

The child got up and shyly shuffled in. To be invited into a warm place full of bread seemed an incredible thing. She did not know what was going to happen to her, exactly.

"Get yourself warm, first," said the baker woman, pointing to a fire in the tiny back room of the shop. "And look here. When you can't get a bit of bread, you can come in here and ask for some. I'm blessed if I won't give it to you for that young one's sake."

Chapter 9
A Midnight Feast

It was dark when Sara reached the square where the seminary was situated. As she passed the Indian gentleman's house, she could see the usual bright fire glowing in the grate, and the Indian gentleman bundled up in shawls in an armchair in front of it. His head was resting on his hand, and he looked as lonely and as unhappy as ever.

When Sara entered the seminary through the servants' entrance, she ran into Miss Minchin, who had come downstairs to scold the cook. "Where have you been wasting your time?" she demanded of Sara as soon as she saw her. "You have been out for hours!"

"It was so wet and muddy that it was hard to walk," Sara replied calmly. "My shoes are so worn out that I kept slipping."

"Make no excuses," snapped Miss Minchin, "and tell no lies."

Miss Minchin stalked back upstairs, and Sara went into the kitchen. The cook had just experienced Miss Minchin's hot temper, too. She was in a terrible mood as a result. Sara was the most convenient person to vent her anger upon at that moment. "You're back so late. Why didn't you just stay out all night, while you were at it?" the cook said sarcastically.

Sara laid her heavy basket of groceries on the table. "Here is everything you wrote down on your list," Sara said mildly.

The cook looked over the packages, grumbling. She was in a very bad temper, indeed.

"May I have something to eat?" Sara asked, faint with hunger.

"Supper's over and done with," was Cook's answer. "I suppose you expected me to save you a plate and keep it hot for you, too?"

Sara stood, silent, for a second. "I have had nothing to eat today but a hot bun," she said.

"There's some bread in the pantry. That's all you'll get at this time of night."

Sara went and found the bread. It was old and hard and dry, but she ate it as she dragged herself up the three flights of stairs to her room. She intended to put herself to bed, hoping that sleep would make her forget her rumbling stomach.

When Sara finally reached the top landing and paused to rest her wobbly legs once more, she saw a glimmer of light coming from underneath her door. That meant that Ermengarde had managed to slip upstairs to pay her a visit. Sara was glad of the company. The mere presence of plump, comfortable Ermengarde, wrapped against the cold in her red wool shawl, would warm the room and lift her spirits a little.

"Oh, you do look tired, Sara," Ermengarde exclaimed as Sara entered the room. "You are quite pale."

"I am tired," Sara admitted, dropping

onto the lopsided footstool. "I didn't expect to see you tonight, Ermie."

"Papa has sent me some more books. There they are," Ermengarde said, pointing unhappily.

For a moment, Sara forgot her troubles. "How wonderful! Carlyle's *French Revolution*. I have been wanting to read this!"

"I haven't! All these big, fat, difficult

books!" Ermengarde wailed. "Papa will be so upset if I don't read them all. He'll expect me to know all about them when I go home for the holidays. He'll quiz me on them. Oh, what am I going to do?"

"Look here," Sara cried excitedly. "If you lend me these books, I will read them for you. I will tell you everything that is in them—I'll teach them to you so that you won't forget anything!"

"Take them, then! I wish I wanted them, but I don't. I'm just not interested in them, but my father is, and he thinks I ought to be, too!"

"What are you going to tell your father if he asks you where you have put your new books?"

"Oh, he won't ask. He'll think I've read them. He doesn't have to know the truth."

"But we would be lying! And, lies—well, you see, lies are not only wicked. Lies are vulgar. Sometimes, I have thought about doing something wicked—like I might fly into a rage and kill Miss Minchin, you know, when she was scolding and insulting me—but I could never stand being vulgar. Why can't you tell your father that you gave them to me?"

"He wants me to read them. He wants me to know what's in them."

"But if I can make you remember what is in them by telling you stories that bring the events to life for you, would he be satisfied with that?"

"He'll like it if I learn anything in any way," Ermengarde moaned impatiently. "You would, too, if you were my father."

Suddenly, both girls froze, as they heard Miss Minchin's voice floating up the steps. Sara sprang up from her stool to put out the candle. It was very rare that Miss Minchin came up the last flight of stairs. Sara had known her to do it only once before. But now she seemed to be angry enough to be coming at least part of the way up. It sounded as if she were driving Becky up the steps in front of her.

"You dishonest, thieving child! Cook tells me that food has been found missing from the pantry many times before now, too!"

"'Twarn't me, mum," sobbed Becky. "I was hungry enough, sure, but 'twarn't me—never!"

"Half a meat pie, indeed! You should be sent to prison!"

"'Twarn't me," wept Becky. "I could've ate a whole one—but I never laid a finger on it."

"Don't tell lies. Get in your room this instant. And no dinner or supper for you tomorrow!" Miss Minchin yelled as she stomped back downstairs.

Sara and Ermengarde heard Becky shut the door of her room and throw herself sobbing upon her bed. Sara could scarcely stand still, but she dared not move until Miss Minchin had retreated and all was still.

"That wicked, cruel woman!" Sara burst forth when it was safe to do so. "The cook takes things herself for her boyfriend and then says Becky steals them. Becky doesn't steal! She's so hungry sometimes that she eats crusts out of the ash barrel, but she doesn't steal!"

Sara fell to the floor and broke into passionate sobs, her hands pressed hard against her face. Sara was crying! The unconquerable Sara! This was a side of Sara that Ermengarde had never seen before. An awful possibility dawned on her all at once. "Sara," she asked in a timid voice as she relit their candle, "are—are—you never told me—please don't think I'm rude for asking, but—do you ever go without enough to eat? Do you ever go hungry, like Becky?"

It was too much just at that moment. The barrier broke down. Sara lifted her face from her hands. "Yes! Yes, I do!" she cried. "I'm so hungry now that I could almost eat you! And it makes it worse to hear poor Becky crying in there. She's hungrier than I am."

Ermengarde gasped. "Oh, Sara! Why didn't you tell me?"

"I did not want you to know. It would have made me feel like a beggar. It is bad enough to look like one now. I know I do."

"No, you don't!"

"Yes, I do. A little boy once gave me a sixpence for charity." Sara pulled out the sixpence on its ribbon from under the collar of her dress. "He would not have given me his sixpence if I had not looked like I had needed it."

Somehow, the sight of the dear gift cheered Sara up, and she started laughing through her tears.

"Who was he?" Ermengarde inquired.

"One of the Large Family—the one I call Guy Clarence. I suppose his nursery was crammed with Christmas presents and with baskets full of cakes and sweets. He could see I had nothing."

"Oh, Sara!" Ermengarde cried. "What a

slow-witted creature I am not to have thought of it before! This very afternoon, my aunt sent me a box filled with good things to eat! It's got cakes in it, and buns, and oranges, and figs, and chocolate! I'll creep downstairs to my room and get it this minute, and we'll eat it all now! Go get Becky!"

By the time Ermengarde came back, Sara and Becky had done their best to give Sara's room the look and feel of a party. Ermengarde's red shawl served as a tablecloth. Sara had found some old lace handkerchiefs, forgotten in a corner of her now-empty trunk, and had laid them around the table to serve as plates and napkins. Some of the red tissue paper that had enveloped the handkerchiefs had been wadded up to look like a fire in the grate. Sara had also found a few silk flowers around an old straw hat. The flowers now adorned the soap dish, which served as a centerpiece for the table.

"What a lovely table!" Ermengarde exclaimed as she set down her hamper.

"Isn't it nice?" Sara agreed. "Somehow, something always happens just before things get too awful to bear. It is as if some sort of magic transforms things. The worst thing never quite comes!"

"And, oh, Miss Ermengarde! Wait till Sara's told you what everythin' is!

These aren't just—oh, please tell her about the banquet hall!" Becky begged.

And so, as they unpacked the feast from the hamper, Sara began a story in which they were all princesses in a magnificent banquet hall. An enormous fire blazed in the grate, warming the huge room. Torches glinted along the walls, and rich, soft carpets lay everywhere underfoot. Golden plates graced the table, as well as an immense bouquet of flowers displayed in a bowl encrusted with precious gemstones.

None of the girls noticed the smiling face of the white-turbaned Ram Dass gazing at them from a corner of Sara's skylight, looking down at them like a guardian angel.

"Advance, fair damsels, and take your places at the banquet table," Sara said graciously. "My noble father, the king, who is absent on a long journey, has sent word commanding us to feast together in his honor. What ho! There,

minstrels! Strike up with your harps
and lutes, and play sweet music for us!
Ah, that's wonderful! And now, let us
begin."

Sara had just passed around the first
plate of cake when they all heard
someone coming up the stairs. The girls
sprang to their feet and turned pale
faces to the door—listening—listening.
There was no mistake about it. Each of
them recognized the angry tread

mounting the stairs, and knew that the end of all good things had come.

"It's—the missus!" choked Becky, dropping her piece of cake on the floor. Miss Minchin struck open the door with a blow of her hand. She was pale with rage.

"My aunt sent me the hamper. We're only having a party!" Ermengarde howled.

"In the middle of the night! A secret party, while everyone's sleeping! And you have brought your beautiful new books up into this dirty attic. Take them back

to your room, where you will stay all day tomorrow. I shall write to your father. What would he say if he knew where you were when you should have been in bed! And here," Miss Minchin concluded as she dumped the feast in a jumbled heap back into the hamper, "take this with you."

Something in Sara's serious, fixed gaze made Miss Minchin turn to her next. "What are you thinking of?" she demanded fiercely. "Why do you look at me that way?"

"I was wondering what my father would say if he knew where I was tonight."

"You horrid, unmanageable child. How dare you! Get into bed this instant! And you," she screamed at Becky, "go to your room at once!"

As Becky stumbled from Sara's room, Miss Minchin turned to follow her out. "I will leave you to your wonderings," she said sarcastically as she slammed the door behind her.

Sara's banquet dream had come to a terrible, nightmarish end. The table was left bare, and the musicians in the gallery had crept away unseen, like mice. Emily was sitting with her back against the wall, staring very hard. Sara picked up her doll with trembling hands. "There isn't any banquet left, Emily. And there aren't any princesses. Nothing but prisoners starving in the Bastille." And she sat down on the floor and hid her head against Emily's chest for a long, long time. She always sat like that, hunched over her knees, when she was trying to bear something in silence.

Finally, Sara got up and went to bed. "I cannot pretend anything else today—there is no use trying. If I go to sleep, perhaps a dream will come and pretend for me." Sara suddenly felt extremely tired—because she was so hungry. "Suppose there was a bright fire in the grate, with lots of little dancing flames," she murmured. "Suppose there was a comfortable chair before it,

and a small table, with a hot supper on it. And suppose"—she yawned as she pulled the thin coverlet up under her chin—"suppose this was a really soft bed, with fleecy blankets and big feather pillows. Suppose—suppose..." And her weariness felt good to Sara as she closed her eyes and fell fast asleep.

Chapter 10
The Magic

Sara woke up before morning dawned. She had no idea how long she had slept. She was not quite sure what had awakened her, although she vaguely remembered hearing something like the sound of her skylight clicking shut.

At first, Sara did not open her eyes. She felt too sleepy. Curiously enough, she also felt warm and comfortable in her bed, for what seemed like the first time in her life in the attic. She was so warm and comfortable that she did not quite believe that she was really awake.

"What a nice dream," she murmured. It must have been a dream. She could feel many warm blankets heaped upon her. When she put out her hand, she touched something exactly like a satin-covered down comforter. There was a light dancing before her closed eyelids, like the light from a merry little fire in the grate.

Sara's eyes opened in spite of her best efforts to keep them shut, to prolong the dream. And then she actually smiled, for what she saw she had never seen in her attic before. "Oh, I have not yet awakened," she whispered, daring to rise on her elbow and look all around her. "I am dreaming still."

Spread on the floor before a blazing
fire lay a thick red rug. On this rug, a
folding chair, unfolded, supported a
comfortable pillow. Next to the chair, a
small folding table, also unfolded, held
several covered serving dishes on a
white cloth. There were cups, saucers, a
teapot bubbling over the fire in the
grate, and a lamp giving out soft light for
reading under a rosy shade. Sara saw
new blankets on her bed, and a silk robe
and a pair of slippers waiting for her at
the foot of the bed.

Sara sat up. Her breathing came short and fast. "It does not—melt away!" she gasped. "I have never had such a dream before. I am dreaming—I am getting out of bed," she heard her own voice say. She stood up in the middle of her transformed room and walked slowly toward the fire in the grate. "I am dreaming, yet it stays real! The fire is really hot! It is bewitched—or I am bewitched."

Sara touched the table, the dishes, and the rug. She put on the dressing gown and slipped into her slippers. "These are real, too. It is all real, wonderfully real!" she cried. "I am not—I am not dreaming."

Sara almost staggered to the books waiting for her on the cushion of the chair. She opened the one on top. Something was written inside the cover—just a few words. "To the little girl in the attic. From a friend." Sara put her face down on the book and burst into tears. "I do not know who it is," she sobbed, "but somebody cares for me a little after all. I do have friends."

Four knocks on the wall brought Becky to Sara's room. Sara drew the speechless girl into the warm, glowing space. "It's true. It is true!" Sara reassured her friend. "I have touched everything. Everything you see is as real

as we are. The Magic has come and done this, Becky, while we were asleep— the Magic that will not let those worst things ever quite happen."

Imagine what the next hour was like. Becky and Sara knelt by the fire blazing in the grate. They removed the covers of the dishes, and found rich, savory soup and sandwiches and muffins enough for both of them. The tea was so delicious that it was unnecessary to pretend that it was anything else but tea. The two

girls were finally warm and fully fed and happy.

As sleep overpowered them, Sara gave Becky half the new blankets, and each girl retired to her bed, to sleep for the few short hours before dawn. Becky turned as she left Sara's room, and took one last look with devouring eyes. "If it ain't here in the mornin', miss," she said sighing, "it's been here tonight, anyways, an' I shall never forget it."

The next morning, Sara hurried down to the kitchen. She had overslept a little, and so had not yet seen Becky that day. She found her friend in the scullery, scrubbing a kettle and humming a happy little tune to herself. Becky looked up at Sara with a wildly happy face. "They were there when I woke up, miss—the blankets, I mean," she whispered excitedly. "As real as they were last night!"

"So were mine!" Sara crowed. "It is all up there now—all of it. While I was

dressing, I ate some of the cold things we left over."

"Oh, laws! Oh, laws!" Becky uttered the exclamation in a sort of delighted groan. She ducked her head over her kettle just in time to hide her smile as the cook came in to send Sara out on the morning's errands.

If it were possible for weather to be worse than it had been the day before, it was worse—wetter, muddier, colder. There were more errands to be done. The cook was even more irritable. Knowing that

Sara was in trouble with Miss Minchin, made her meaner than ever.

It was quite late when Sara was at last able to go upstairs to her room. She had spent some time in the schoolroom, studying after her workday had ended. When Sara reached the top flight of stairs and stood before the attic door, her heart beat rather fast.

"Of course, all of it might have been taken away during the course of the day," she whispered, trying to be brave. "It might have been lent to me briefly, for just that one awful night. But it was indeed mine for a night—I had it! It was all real!"

Sara pushed open the door and went

in. The Magic had been there again! It had done even more than before! A lovely piece of heavy, embroidered cloth covered the mantel. The bare, ugly walls had been covered with draperies and small pictures and made to look quite

pretty. Brilliantly colored fans had been pinned up, and there were several large cushions, large enough to use as seats, scattered on the floor. Sara's old trunk had been covered with a thick rug, and some cushions had been placed on it, to give it quite the air of a real sofa. Best of all, dinner for two was waiting for Sara and Becky in front of another merrily burning fire in the grate.

"This is exactly like a fairy tale come true," Sara gasped. "There is not the least little bit of difference. I feel as if I might wish for anything—diamonds or bags of gold—and they would just appear! That would not be any more strange than what is happening right now! Is this my room? Am I the same cold, ragged, damp, and muddy Sara? And to think I used to wish there were fairies! I am living in a fairy story—why, I might have become a fairy myself!"

Sara knocked on the wall for Becky, who almost dropped in a heap upon the floor when she arrived. "Oh, laws!" she cried. "Oh, laws, miss! Where does it all come from? Who does it, miss?"

"Let us not even ask!" Sara replied. "I would certainly like to thank whoever it is, but otherwise I would rather not know. It makes it all the more beautiful, don't you think?"

From that time on, life for the two girls became more wonderful day by day. The fairy story continued. Almost every day, something new was added to Sara's room—a folding bookshelf filled with books, a writing case with pens and paper, new comforts and conveniences of all kinds, until there seemed nothing left to be desired. When Sara went downstairs in the morning, the remains of the previous evening's supper were on the table. When she returned to the attic at night, the Magic had removed the dishes and left another nice meal. The comfort and happiness she and Becky enjoyed were making them stronger.

Sara began to look less thin, and her
eyes did not seem that much too big for
her face any longer. Becky was
beginning to look healthier and much
happier, too.

Then another mysterious thing
happened. A delivery man came to the
door and left several packages. All of
them were addressed in large letters "To
the Little Girl in the Right-Hand Attic."
Sara had been sent to the door when the
delivery man rang the bell. She was still
looking in astonishment at the address
labels on the parcels, when Miss
Minchin came into the front hall and
found her. "Don't just stand there gawk-
ing," Miss Minchin said impatiently.
"Take the packages to the young lady to
whom they belong."

"They belong to me," Sara replied,
smiling.

"To you? What on earth do you mean?"

"I do not know where they come from,
but they are addressed to me. I am the

girl who sleeps in the right-hand attic room. Becky has the other one."

"What is in the parcels?"

"I do not know."

"Well, open them, then!" Miss Minchin ordered.

Sara did as she was told. Out tumbled pretty and practical clothing—dresses, warm stockings, gloves, shoes, and a warm, long coat. There were even a nice hat and a sturdy umbrella. These items were all good and expensive, the clothes well-made and perfectly tailored, just the right size for Sara. On the pocket of the coat was pinned a paper that said, "To Be Worn Every Day—Will Be Replaced By Others When Necessary."

Miss Minchin frowned. Could it be that she had made a mistake in believing Sara to be truly orphaned? Perhaps some relative had suddenly chosen to provide for Sara in this mysterious way. Relations were

sometimes very odd, particularly rich, old uncles who did not care to have young children near them. Such a person would not be pleased to find out the truth about the shabby clothes, the inadequate food, and the rough work

Miss Minchin had provided for what she thought had been a charity case, hers to do with as she saw fit.

"Well," said Miss Minchin uncertainly. "Since the things have been sent, you may as well go put them on. After you are dressed, you may come down to the schoolroom. You need not go out on any more errands today."

That night, after supper with Becky in her room, Sara sat looking at the fire. "Are you makin' up somethin' in your head, miss?" Becky inquired respectfully.

"No, I am wondering what I ought to do. I cannot help but think about our friends, the fairies," Sara explained. "If they want to keep their identity a secret, it would be impolite of us to try to find out who they are. But I do so want to let them know how grateful we are. Anyone who is kind and generous likes to hear that people have been made happy by such generosity. Benefactors care more

for that than for being thanked. I do wish"— Sara paused as her eyes fell upon her writing case—"oh!" she continued. "Why didn't I think of that before? I can write to them, and leave my note on the table. Then perhaps the fairies who clear the supper dishes will take my note, too. I will not ask them anything—they won't mind my writing, I feel sure!"

Sara wrote a note, which said, "I hope you will not think me rude for writing this message when you might wish to keep your identity a secret. Please believe that I do not mean to be impolite. I do not seek to know anything at all about the Magic. I only want to thank you for being so kind to me and to Becky. We used to be so lonely and cold and hungry, and now—oh, just think what you have done for us! Thank you so very much! Your friend, The Little Girl in the Attic."

Chapter 11

Lost and Found

Sara had left her note on the table, hoping it would get taken and delivered with the supper dishes. Sure enough, that evening when she came back to her room, the note was gone. The Magicians had received her thanks, and Sara was happier for the thought.

Sara was reading one of her new books aloud to Becky just before bedtime, when her attention was attracted by a sound at the skylight.

When she looked up from her page, she saw that Becky had heard the sound also.

"Somethin's there, miss," Becky said nervously.

"It sounds rather like a cat, on the roof, trying to get in."

Sara went to the skylight. It was a queer little sound she heard, like a soft scratching. She climbed on a chair, very cautiously opened the skylight, and peeped out. It had been snowing all day.

On the new-fallen snow, quite near her, crouched a tiny, shivering creature.

"It is the monkey that belongs to Ram Dass," Sara cried.

"Who is Ram Dass?" Becky asked.

"The Lascar—I mean the manservant of the English gentleman next door. Servants who are men are called Lascars in India."

"Are you goin' to let the monkey in, miss?" Becky asked in a frightened voice.

"Oh, yes! It is much too cold for monkeys to be outside. They are very delicate creatures. He must have crept out of the other attic and come here when he saw our light. Help me coax him inside."

Sara put her hand out and spoke to the monkey as she often spoke to the sparrows when she fed them, as if she, too, were some friendly little animal who understood his timid wildness. "Come along, monkey darling," she cooed. "I would never hurt you." Sara laid her hand gently on his back and drew him toward her. The monkey had felt this kind of human love in the slim brown hands of Ram Dass. He now felt the same tender affection in Sara's hands. He let her lift him through the skylight. When he found himself in her arms, he clung closely to her and took friendly hold of a lock of her hair.

The monkey was evidently glad to get to the fire. When Sara sat down and held him on her knee, he looked from her to Becky with interest and appreciation. "Nice monkey! Nice monkey," Sara crooned as she petted his funny head. "I love little animals like you so much!"

"He is plain-lookin', miss, ain't he?" Becky remarked, doubtful that she would ever want to hold such a thing.

"He does indeed look like a very ugly baby."

"What are you goin' to do with him, miss?"

"I shall let him sleep at the bottom of my bed tonight. Tomorrow morning, I will take him back to the Indian gentleman, first thing." When she and Becky said good night a short while later, the monkey made for himself a nest of Sara's robe at the foot of the bed, and curled up at her feet as if he were very pleased to be spending the night there.

The next morning, Sara slipped out of the seminary with the monkey under

her coat. When she arrived at the Indian
gentleman's house, Ram Dass seemed
delighted to see both her and the
monkey. He quickly ushered Sara into
his master's study.

Sara entered the room with the
monkey in her arms. The creature
evidently did not intend to be parted
from his new friend, if it could be
helped. He clung to Sara and chattered
away. The excitement of finding both the
Indian gentleman and the father of the
Large Family together, in the same
warm room she had so often gazed at
from outside the window, brought a
flush to Sara's cheeks.

"Your monkey ran away again, sir,"
Sara said as she curtsied prettily. "He
came to my window late last night. I
took him in right away because it was so
cold. I would have brought him back to
you immediately if it had not been so
late. I did not wish to disturb you."

"That was very thoughtful of you,"

replied the invalid by the fire. The gentleman's hollow eyes dwelt upon Sara with a sort of intense curiosity or interest.

Sara looked toward Ram Dass, who stood near the door. "Shall I give the monkey to your Lascar?" she asked.

"How do you know he is a Lascar?" the gentleman inquired, smiling slightly.

"I was born in India," Sara replied simply.

The Indian gentleman sat bolt upright so suddenly in his chair, and had such a change of expression on his face, that Sara was quite startled. "You were born in India, you say? But you live next door!" Something seemed to be the matter.

"Yes, I live at Miss Minchin's Select Seminary for Young Ladies."

"But you are not one of her pupils?"

"I do not know exactly what I am at the present time."

"Why not? What do you mean?"

"At first, I was a pupil, a parlor-boarder, but now—"

"You were once a pupil? What are you, now?"

"I sleep in the attic. I run errands. I do anything anyone asks, and I teach the little ones their lessons in French and in history."

"Question her, Carmichael," the Indian gentleman said suddenly to the father of the Large Family. "Ask her

everything, down to the last detail. I
have not the strength to do it. The
excitement is too much for me right
now. I feel ill." The Indian gentleman
collapsed back into the depths of his
armchair. Ram Dass brought his
master a glass of water.

"What do you mean by 'at first,' my
child?" began Mr. Carmichael with an
encouraging smile.

"When I was first taken to the
seminary by my papa."

"Where is your papa now?"

"He died," Sara said very quietly. "He lost all of his money, and so there was none left for me. There was no one to take care of me or to pay Miss Minchin for my room and board."

"How did your father lose his money?" the Indian man broke in, gasping for breath.

"He did not lose it himself. He had a friend he was very fond of—he was very fond of him, and he trusted him. It was his friend who took his money. He trusted his friend too much."

"But the friend did not mean to do him harm! It happened through a mistake!" the Indian man said.

"The suffering was just as bad for my father," Sara replied. "It killed him. He died of brain fever."

"What was your father's name! Tell me! I cannot bear it!"

"His name was Ralph Crewe," Sara answered, feeling very startled and strange. "He died in India two years ago."

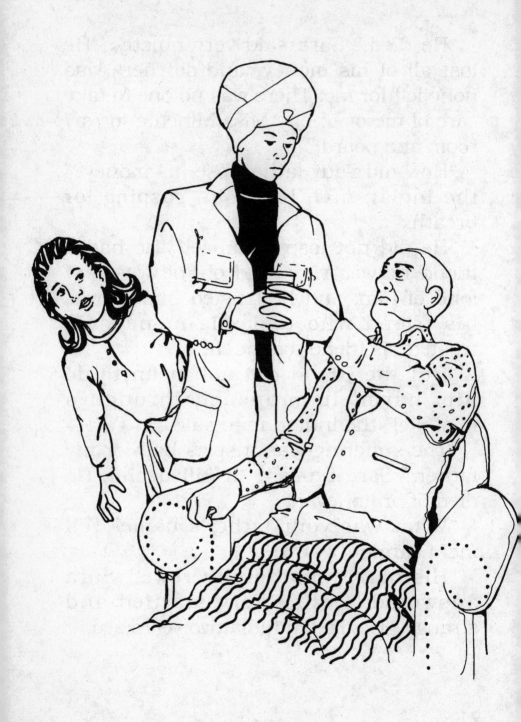

"Carmichael!" the invalid gasped. "It is the child—the child, his child! We have found her at last!"

For a moment, Sara thought the Indian gentleman was going to die. Ram Dass leaped to his master's side, with another glass of water.

Sara stood nearby, trembling a little. She looked in a bewildered way at Mr. Carmichael. "What child am I?" she faltered.

"This gentleman is Mr. Carrisford, your father's friend. When it seemed that the diamond mines were failing, he became ill with fever, like your father did. Mr. Carrisford was taken to the hospital, where he lay raving mad with fever for weeks. Unfortunately, when he recovered, he remembered very little of what had happened. The fever had given him amnesia, you see, erasing much of his memory. He knew your father had died, and could not forgive himself. But he remembered little else. The rest of his memory came back slowly and in pieces. By the time he remembered that Ralph Crewe had spoken to him of his little girl in boarding school, six months had passed. No matter how hard he tried, he could not remember where your father had said the school was located. We have been looking for you in every major city in Europe, as far away as Russia! And now, at last, we have found you! Or, rather, you have found us!"

Sara put her hand up to her forehead. Her mouth trembled as her eyes filled with tears. She spoke as if she were dreaming. "And I was at Miss Minchin's all the while," she said feebly. "Just on the other side of the wall."

Chapter 12

Anne

Mr. Carrisford had fainted from the shock of finally encountering Sara. When he regained consciousness, he looked around wildly to see her, and then fell back against his chair in relief when he glimpsed her sitting near Ram Dass and the monkey. "I am so sorry, Sara darling," he wept as he held out his arms to her. "I am not a wicked man. I have been punished for my foolishness. I have sent Mr. Carmichael to the far corners of the earth looking for you.

Thank heavens we have found you at last! My little girl in the right-hand attic," he murmured as he hugged her to him. With one hand, he fished in the breast pocket of his robe. He pulled out Sara's note of thanks. He had been keeping it close to his heart.

"It was you who brought the Magic?" Sara said, looking at him in astonishment.

"I could not have done it without Ram Dass. He told me about you. We figured out together this way of helping you. It was Ram Dass who was strong and agile and quiet enough to get the things I chose for you into your room."

"But why did you do it?"

"I did it for Sara Crewe's sake. I had no idea that you were Sara Crewe, but I could not stand the thought of another poor, penniless girl struggling without anyone to help or care for her. In my delirium, after my terrible bout with brain fever, I had left my friend's only daughter in that perilous, penniless state."

"Then it is you who are my friend!" Sara cried, throwing her arms around Mr. Carrisford's neck. "You and Ram Dass. You have been a true friend to my father!" Sara kissed her friend lovingly on the cheek.

"The man will be himself again in a matter of weeks," predicted Mr. Carmichael. "You can see the difference in his face already!"

In fact, Tom Carrisford did indeed look and feel like a new man. There were many things to think of and to plan. Sara was not to return to the seminary at all. He was adamant about that. Mr. Carmichael was to draft a letter to Miss Minchin explaining in legal terms all that had happened and outlining Sara's changed fortunes. Becky was to be sent next door to the town house, where Mr. Carrisford proposed to hire her as Sara's personal maid and companion. No more pots to scrub! And plenty to eat!

Moreover, Miss Minchin must be informed that any girl from the seminary whom Sara considered a friend was to be allowed to visit Sara at her new home next door. If Miss Minchin objected to any of this, she was to be told that to mistreat or to otherwise interfere in the happiness of Sara Crewe, heiress of millions from the recovered diamond mines, would surely reflect badly on her seminary. The parents of Miss Crewe's friends were not likely to refuse invitations to visit her at her guardian's house. Stories of the shameful way Miss Minchin had treated her former charity pupil would be circulated by Mr. Carrisford to all these parents, if necessary.

In a month's time, Tom Carrisford had fully recovered from his illness and his depression. He had never met anyone he liked quite as much as he loved his adopted daughter, Sara. There were so many charming things for the Magicians of the house to do to surprise and delight her. There might be beautiful fresh flowers to place in her room, or small gifts to tuck under her pillow. Once, as they sat together in the evening, they heard the scratch of a heavy paw on the door. When Sara went to find out what it was, there stood an enormous dog—a splendid Russian boarhound—wearing a collar bearing the words, "I am Boris. I serve the Princess Sara."

The hours when Sara and the Indian gentleman sat alone reading or talking had a special charm of their own. One evening, as Mr. Carrisford looked up from his book, he saw that his companion sat gazing into the fire. "What are you 'supposing,' Sara?" he inquired.

"I was supposing," she said, "I was remembering that hungry day, and a child I saw outside."

"But there were a great many hungry days. Which one was it?"

"The day the Magic first came." Then,

Sara told her guardian the story of the bakery, and of the fourpence she picked up out of the mud, and the beggar child. She told it quite simply, and in as few words as possible. "I was also supposing a kind of plan," she continued. "I was thinking I would like to do something."

"And what would that be?" asked Mr. Carrisford, curious. "You may do anything you like."

"I was wondering," said Sara shyly. "I was wondering if I could go to see the bun-woman, and tell her that—if, when hungry children—particularly on those dreadfully cold days—come sit on her steps, or look in the window, if she would just call them in and feed them, and then she could send the bills to me. Could I do that?"

"You shall do it tomorrow morning."

"Thank you. You see, I know what it is to be hungry. It is very hard when you cannot even pretend your hunger away."

The next morning, a carriage drew
up before the door of Brown's Bakery.
Its occupants descended just as Mrs.
Brown was putting a tray of
smoking-hot buns into the window
display. She looked at Sara closely as
she entered her shop, and then her
good-natured face lit up in recognition.
"I'm sure that I remember you, miss,"
she exclaimed. "And yet—"

"You once gave me six buns for
fourpence. Today's special," Sara said,
winking.

"And you gave five of them to a beggar child. I've always remembered it. I
beg your pardon, sir," she said, turning
to Mr. Carrisford, "but there aren't
many young people who notice a hungry face in that way. Excuse the liber-
ty, miss—but you look rosier and, well,
better, healthier, than you did that
day."

"I am better, thank you," Sara replied.
"And I am much happier, too. I have

Treasury of Illustrated Classics

Adventures of Huckleberry Finn
The Adventures of Pinocchio
The Adventures of Robin Hood
The Adventures of Sherlock Holmes
The Adventures of Tom Sawyer
Alice in Wonderland
Anne of Green Gables
Beauty and the Beast
Black Beauty
The Call of the Wild
Frankenstein
Great Expectations
Gulliver's Travels
Heidi
Jane Eyre
Journey to the Center of the Earth
The Jungle Book
King Arthur and the Knights of the Round Table
The Legend of Sleepy Hollow & Rip Van Winkle
A Little Princess
Little Women
Moby Dick
Oliver Twist
Peter Pan
The Prince and the Pauper
Pygmalion
Rebecca of Sunnybrook Farm
Robinson Crusoe
The Secret Garden
Swiss Family Robinson
The Time Machine
Treasure Island
20,000 Leagues Under the Sea
White Fang
The Wind in the Willows
The Wizard of Oz